JACK KENT

Hoddy Doddy

Greenwillow
Read·alone

GREENWILLOW BOOKS
A Division of William Morrow & Company, Inc., New York

TO HONEY AND WES

Library of Congress Cataloging in Publication Data
Kent, Jack (date)   Hoddy doddy.
(Greenwillow read-alone books)
Summary: Presents three Danish tales of foolish
fellows: The Lobsters, The Clock, and The Patriot.
1. Tales, Danish.   [1. Folklore—Denmark]
I. Title.   PZ8.1.K416Ho   [398.2]   [E]   78-23635
ISBN 0-688-80192-7   ISBN 0-688-84192-9 lib. bdg.

Contents

The Lobsters

In a little town in Denmark
there lived an old hoddy doddy
(that is to say, a foolish fellow)
and his wife.
They had a pastry shop.

Every day people came
to buy the good things
that were for sale.
While choosing six of those
and a dozen of these,
they would visit a little
and tell the news.

One day the news was

that a ship from Norway

was in the harbor.

"In all my long life,"
said the old man,
"I have never seen
anybody from Norway."

"Why don't you go to the ship
and visit them?" asked his wife.

"I'll take care of the shop
while you are gone.
Then you can come back and
tell me what they are like."
The old man thanked his wife,
put on his hat and coat,

and went down to the harbor.

"Which is the ship
from Norway?" he asked.
And it was pointed out to him.

The old man couldn't see anybody,

so he went on board the ship.

But he met no one,

for they had all

gone ashore earlier.

Several lobsters that the sailors
had caught had gotten loose
and were creeping
about on the deck.
The old man thought
they were the ship's crew.

"How do you do?" he said.

"I'm pleased to meet you."

    And he went up

    to one of the lobsters

    and gave it his hand to shake.

The lobster grabbed
the old man's hand
and squeezed.

And squeezed!

And SQUEEZED.

The old man howled with pain.

At last the lobster let go.

The old man hurried back
to the pastry shop.

"What are the men from Norway like?"
his wife was eager to know.
"They are rather small people,"
said the old man.

"But they have
a powerful handshake!"

The Clock

The town was in a panic.
Word had just come that
the enemy was headed their way.
Everyone rushed to save
what he could
before the enemy came.

What they thought the most of
was the tower clock.
So that was the first thing
they wanted to save.
They worked long and hard.
At last they got the clock
down from the tower.

"Where shall we hide it
so the enemy
can't find it?"
they asked each other.
"The harbor," someone suggested.

"Sink it in the harbor.

The enemy will never find it there."

So down to the harbor

they went with the clock.

They put the clock in a boat.

Then they rowed way out
where the water was deepest.

There, with a mighty splash,
they dumped the clock.

They watched it sink.

Down, down, down.

"The enemy will never find it there,"
they said.

"But how will we find it
when the enemy has gone?"
one of them asked.

This was the first time any of them
had thought about that.
They puzzled over it for a while
in silence.

Finally one of them spoke.
"The answer is very simple,"
he said.
"All we have to do
is mark the spot."

With that he took a knife
from his pocket and
cut a big X on the side of the boat
where the clock had gone over.

"This is where we threw it overboard,"
he said.

The others nodded.

Then they rowed to shore,
content that now they could
easily find the clock again
when the war was over.

The Patriot

Miller Hansen loved his homeland.
He was certain that
there was none better on earth.

Often, after his work
at the mill was done,
Miller Hansen saddled his horse
and rode through the countryside
just to admire it.

"Are the flowers this beautiful
anywhere else?" he wondered.
"Are the trees this green?
Are the skies this blue?"
He was sure they were not.

People in other places
could not possibly be nicer.
Other cows could not be better.
Other pigs could not be fatter.

Miller Hansen was proud
to be a part
of such a fine land.

One day he was riding
along the border when ahead
of him he heard a cuckoo.

"Nowhere else but here
do cuckoos have such voices,"
said Miller Hansen.
From across the border
another cuckoo
answered the first.
"That's not one of ours,"
the miller said.
He listened as the two birds
took turns cuckooing.
It was soon clear
that they were having a contest
to see which of them
could cuckoo the most.

The miller
got off his horse
and began cheering
for the local bird.

At first it seemed to be winning.

But after a while the miller could tell
that his cuckoo was getting tired.

So Miller Hansen
climbed up the tree
to help out.

The contest went on for hours.

CUCKOO
CUCKOO

And hours.

cuck...

At last the foreign bird
was forced to give up.
It could cuckoo
no more.

When the folks back home
heard about the victory,
they gave Miller Hansen
a hero's welcome.

A statue in memory
of the event was raised
in the town square.
And there it stands
to this very day.

MILLER
HANSEN
PATRIOT

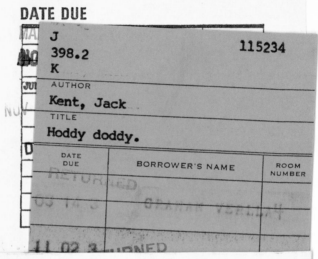